I Say Shehechiyanu

by Joanne Rocklin   Illustrated by Monika Filipina

KAR-BEN
PUBLISHING

For Temple Sinai in Oakland, California, with gratitude, and to my beloved grandchildren. — J.R.

To my baby sister who was my inspiration. —M.F.

KAR-BEN PUBLISHING
A division of Lerner Publishing Group, Inc.
241 First Avenue North
Minneapolis, MN 55401 USA
1-800-4-KARBEN

Website address: www.karben.com

Main body text set in Blockhead Unplugged 16/22.

Library of Congress Cataloging-in-Publication Data

Rocklin, Joanne.
    I say Shehechiyanu / by Joanne Rocklin ; illustrated by Monika Filipina.
       pages   cm.
    ISBN: 978-1-4677-3467-7 (lib. bdg. : alk. paper)
    1. Shehechiyanu—Juvenile literature. 2. Gratitude—Religious aspects—Judaism— Juvenile literature. 3. Benediction—Judaism—Juvenile literature. I. Filipina, Monika, illustrator. II. Title.
    BM670.S44R63 2015
    296.4'5—dc23   2014003570

Manufactured in the United States of America
1 – DP – 12/31/14

A Blessing for Beginnings

"Shehechiyanu" is a Jewish blessing that we say when something takes place for the first time or when it happens again after a long time, and we are thankful to experience it.

Let's say "Shehechiyanu!"

Baruch Atah Adonai, Eloheinu Melech Ha'olam, shehechiyanu vkiy'manu vhigiyanu lazman hazeh.

Blessed are you, Lord our God, Ruler of the Universe, who has granted us life, sustained us, and enabled us to reach this occasion.

Autumn

It's autumn! I say "Shehechiyanu . . ."

On Rosh Hashanah, when the challah is round, and the air smells like apples for a sweet New Year.

When **I** get cool new shoes to celebrate the Jewish New Year.

When my new baby brother holds my finger.

When **I** taste a pomegranate for the very first time.

When **I** run into my new classroom on the first day of school.

And when we eat our first meal
in our sukkah.

Winter

It's winter! I say "Shehechiyanu . . ."

When I light the candles on
the first night of Hanukkah.

When I spin the dreidel, and when I
teach someone else to spin it, too.

When my baby brother grows a new tooth.

When the first big snow comes
and I am snug and warm, inside.

When guests come for Shabbat dinner.

When **I** see the full moon and it is so clear
and round **I** can almost see footprints on it.

Spring

It's spring! I say "Shehechiyanu..."

When I hear a bird singing, "I'm back!"

When I see a curled up bud, waiting to open.

When I try on my new Purim costume.

When my baby brother says my name.

When I take my first bite of
matzah at the Passover seder.

And when I am old enough to ask the Four Questions for the first time!

Summer

It's summer! I say "Shehechiyanu . . ."

At the playground, when I surprise myself by winning a race.

When my baby brother takes his first step — right towards me!

When I hear thunder and it doesn't scare me anymore.

When I learn how to braid the challah dough.

When someone I love
has a birthday.

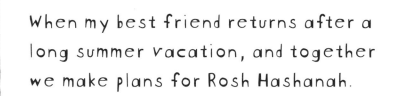

When my best friend returns after a
long summer vacation, and together
we make plans for Rosh Hashanah.

Remembering . . . and imagining . . .

All the "Shehechiyanus."

About the Author and Illustrator

Joanne Rocklin is the author of middle grade novels and early readers. Her previous books include, *The Five Lives of Our Cat Zook*, a Golden Kite Award Winner, *One Day and One Amazing Morning on Orange Street*, and *Fleabrain Loves Franny*. She lives in Oakland, California where she babysits for her grandchildren and makes cakes, cookies, bread, jam, and children's books.

Monika Filipina grew up in the beautiful old city of Thorn, Poland surrounded by cats and other animals that are her main inspiration. After studying Illustration in the United Kingdom, she lives in Thorn with her fiancé and two cats.